Searching for Chessie of the Chesapeake Bay

Story and Illustrations by

Lisa Cole

the Peppertree Press
Sarasota, Florida

For information regarding permission,
call 941-922-2662 or contact us at our website:
www.peppertreepublishing.com or write to:
the Peppertree Press, LLC.
Attention: Publisher
1269 First Street, Suite 7
Sarasota, Florida 34236

ISBN: 978-1-936343-94-2
Library of Congress Number: 2011929011
Printed in the U.S.A.

Printed June 2011

DEDICATION

For Charlie

Table of Contents

Chapter 1

Claire read the sinister sign on her brother's bedroom door. The distinct words were written in a crimson red, "KEEP OUT, NO TRESPASSING." And under the bold words, handwritten in the tiniest, blackest letters were the words, "Especially Claire Meadows." Claire took a deep breath and timidly tapped on the door. She waited for a reply. Then pressing her ear against the door, she heard a muffled-sounding voice from inside the room say, "Enter."

In her hands Claire held an enormously heavy, old faded blue book, worn and terribly frayed around the edges. She gently moved her fingertips over the silky, smooth texture of the gold ornate letters. The letters gave the book the appearance of being ancient and valuable. But the book's outward appearance hardly divulged the importance it held for Claire, for in her hands she held her most secret of secret wishes and her greatest of greatest dreams. Claire opened the door.

Upon entering she was forced to squeeze past stacks of brown dusty boxes containing unread novels, tattered magazines, and a battered collection of video games. Finding the only bare spot on the floor of her brother's bedroom, she plopped down. Anxiously biting her lower lip, she waited for Jim to speak first.

"I give up. What's the book about?" Her brother, Jim, was lying on his rumpled bed surrounded by piles of foul smelling clothes. Ignoring his little sister, he resumed reading a kayaking magazine and flipped through the colorful, glossy pages, glancing at photographs of kayakers gliding through secluded lakes and battling roaring rivers.

Thoughtfully, Claire looked at her brother. His appearance had changed over the past several months. He was leaner and fit. Streaks of blond hair radiated from his thin tanned face, and she could see the faint scar on his nose from a fist fight during summer school. Prior to entering his room, she decided she wasn't going to let his attitude discourage her.

"*The Reality of Legends and Other Unusual Phenomenon,*" she said. Trying to maintain a voice of confidence as she spoke, Claire hoped her brother didn't notice she was trembling. Lately, they were bickering with one another, and Jimmy's solution was to prohibit her from entering his bedroom, giving him the privacy he so desperately needed. The posting of the sign caused her great despair.

"Yeah, so?" He continued flipping through his magazine pausing here and there to look at an advertisement or read a caption.

"Well, you know how we're going to the Chesapeake Bay for kayak camp this summer...," Claire could barely contain her excitement. *Be sensible, not foolish,* she thought.

"Yeah, so?" Acting indifferently towards her usually sent Claire scurrying out of his room, so he continued the attitude.

"There's a story in this book about a sea monster inhabiting the Chesapeake Bay.

The monster's name is..." She hesitated, afraid of what his reaction might be, "... Chessie, her name is Chessie."

Upon hearing the words, 'sea monster,' 'Chesapeake Bay,' and 'Chessie,' startled, he looked up from his magazine. His next reaction was beyond his control—he burst out laughing.

It took him several minutes to regain his composure, as disappointment clouded Claire's face. He could see moisture build on the rims of her eyelids, and her light brown eyes began to glisten as each tear formed a puddle, waiting to be unleashed. He watched as she brushed her dark curly hair aside, trying to control the inevitable.

"Stop laughing at me. If you don't believe me, read for yourself." She hastily handed her brother the heavy book.

Grabbing the book out of her hands, he opened it to the page she had marked and began to read about Chessie. As she suspected, he began to show an interest in the story. "Where did you get this book?"

"I found it at the library. The librarian helped me by using the computer and we stumbled onto some more detailed information. She copied these pages for me. Here—read them."

"Do you see the part where there have been numerous sightings of Chessie? Near Kent Island. That's right across from the kayak camp."

Chapter 2

Jim read the chapter about Chessie and studied the blurry pictures. "Legends are a big bunch of lies. Claire, you're always dreaming. This is just another thing you can daydream about at school. What do you want me to do?" asked Jim as he flipped through the book. "...live in a dream world with you?"

"Chessie is real. There have been several sightings of her in the same area over the past 100 years."

"Claire, listen to me. You know people claim they've seen Sasquatch. There are a million books illustrating pictures of him tramping through the forest and leaving huge imprints of his feet on the ground for people to discover. Funny thing is no one has ever been able to prove, with any real physical evidence, he exists. Everyone knows you have to be loony to believe he's out there."

Jim had read about Sasquatch, the Loch Ness Monster, the Abominable Snowman, and a number of other legendary creatures when he was Claire's age. He was particularly intrigued with two creatures. His favorite was the West Virginia monster, the Winged Mothman. The half-man, half-moth fascinated him. He often thought it would be adventurous to roam mountains in the darkest of night in search of this wonderfully magical monster.

His second favorite was the Skunk Ape of the Florida Everglades. He spent one summer dreaming of searching deep in the heart of the Florida swamp, dodging treacherous alligators to find the elusive creature. *It's all make-believe*, he thought. *Mythical creatures are fake and fabricated in order to scare little children into behaving.* He realized his own foolishness when he tried to share his interest with his friends and they teased him unmercifully about the scary, monstrous creatures.

"Are you positive Sasquatch doesn't

exist?" demanded Claire. "I believe there really is a sea monster named Chessie and she lives in the Chesapeake Bay." Once again, she felt betrayed by her brother. They used to trust each other. They used to share their dreams.

"Well, I guess I could prove to you there isn't one. Do you want to bet on it?"

"Jimmy, there's even a video someone made that proves Chessie exist."

"Bet or no bet—what's it going to be?"

"Bet there is a Chessie!" Claire held out her hand to seal their bet. Neither one of them suggested betting money or making a wager. The thought never crossed their minds. They were betting on who was smarter.

After shaking hands, Claire left the treasured book with her brother and ungraciously stomped out of his room. *He really is impossible*, she thought to herself. *Why did he think she wanted to continue learning to kayak?*

Claire went to her room and opened a map of the Chesapeake Bay. Placing her finger on the point where the camp was located,

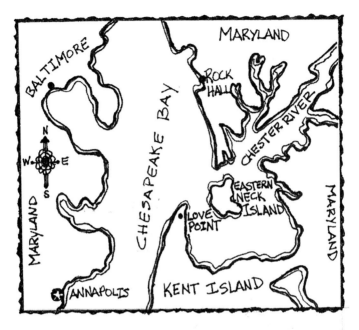

she dragged her finger across to Love Point on Kent Island. It was at Love Point where Chessie was usually spotted between May and September. It was perfect. They would be attending kayaking camp for one week in July.

Chapter 3

Jim was spending most of his afternoons teaching Claire how to kayak in the sparkling, shallow waters on the eastern coast of Florida. Florida became their new home when their mother decided they needed a change in their lives. She packed their belongings and bought a dilapidated silver trailer at a fishing camp.

Each trailer was situated uncomfortably close to the next. The trailers in the camp were so close to each other, they looked like sardines in a tin can. The residents could hear every cough, sneeze, scream, tear, and laugh echo throughout the trailers. There was no privacy. Everyone knew everybody's business.

So it was no surprise when an uninvited audience would position themselves along the wooden dock to gawk at Jim while he gave Claire kayak lessons. And it wasn't surprising when everyone voiced an opinion about his intense instruction. Every time he gave Claire directions, she would become flustered. She didn't know her right from her left and it was becoming a serious problem. Frustrated, she sniffled holding back her tears, which in turn would cause onlookers to approach their mother and tell on him. Understandably their mother, June, would race out to the boat ramp and stand with her hand on her hip glaring at him until he looked at her.

"Don't worry, I'm not hurting her." He spoke first, attempting to reassure her. "I can't help it if she freaks every time she turns turtle in her kayak and can't figure out how to roll it upright. I've tried to show her at least a hundred times. Mom, she's got to toughen up a little."

"Junior, remember she's only ten years old." Jim cringed when he heard her say, 'Junior.' He despised the nickname and she knew it. He directed Claire to follow him.

"You're the one who wants her to learn how to kayak." He grabbed his kayak and dragging it up into the clumps of faded marsh grass lining the shore, he beached it. He walked away disgusted.

Their mother spent a great deal of time and expense searching for an activity her children could do together. Since their father's departure, Jim's mother asked him to assume more responsibility in the family. This meant keeping a watchful eye on Claire.

Claire had a tendency to disappear. Generally, she was nearby playing with a friend or fishing on the dock and her disappearances were harmless. But Claire was told time and time again to leave a brief note on the family bulletin board for safety purposes. The family's "note rule" was strictly enforced, and her refusal to follow it was disturbing their mother. Jim hated his newly assigned responsibility.

"Jimmy, come back—I'll learn." Claire brushed the tears off her sunburned cheeks as she fumbled with her paddle.

Grudgingly, he continued to teach her. He demonstrated how to release a spray skirt, pull out of the kayak quickly and grab hold of it, then use it as a floatation device. Claire didn't understand how to roll her kayak and turn upright while seated, but she could manage the wet exit from her kayak if it flipped upside-down in the water.

"When you wet exit, try to keep one hand firmly on the kayak. Grip it so it doesn't drift away," he instructed her. "Be careful not to let it hit your head." Jim watched Claire practice several times in shallow water. Then they paddled into deeper water and after several attempts of struggling to perfect the technique, she was successful.

"Jimmy, wet exits scare me. I get water in my nose."

"If you don't learn how to exit your kayak, you'll never learn how to roll it. So either way, you're going to have to learn how to survive if your boat turns over. I won't always be there to rescue you," said Jim.

Rubbing her sore nose, Claire decided to keep her discomfort a secret from her brother.

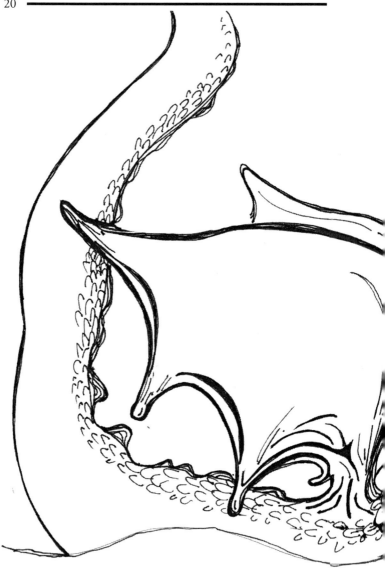

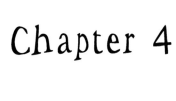

Chapter 4

The day before they left for kayak camp at Eastern Neck Island in Maryland, Jim told Claire they needed special equipment to search for the sea monster. Every time Jim said, "Chessie," he cracked up, practically splitting his sides laughing. One time he laughed so hard tears filled his eyes and he had to gasp for air. Claire was growing increasingly discouraged.

"Seriously," said Jim, in between fits of laughter. "...we'll probably have to sneak out of camp at about four o'clock in the morning so we can return by six o'clock for breakfast. We have to give ourselves plenty of time to dry off and stow our gear. No one will ever suspect we went out on the water."

"What do we need to take with us?" asked Claire.

Jimmy thought for a moment. "We need two head lamps and one waterproof box camera. Who's going to ask Mom to buy the stuff? She's going to ask a lot of questions."

"I will," offered Claire. "I'll tell her it's for an extra trip the camp is planning."

Claire found her mother perched on an old dingy white stool at the counter in the fishing camp's bait shop. She was talking to Captain Jack about a recent fishing charter. Claire handed the list to her mother and explained how the camp was offering an extra kayak trip for experienced paddlers.

"Sounds like you'll be going on a night paddle. I'll pick up the equipment for you, June," said Captain Jack. He was always eager to assist their mother. "Claire, get Jimmy and I'll drive you two over to the store."

Once Claire and Jim were in Captain Jack's rusty blue truck, he began to jabber nonstop about his days as a waterman on the Chesapeake Bay and how his family prospered there for generations. He described, in detail, his younger years running boats and picking up crab pots. He recounted the horrifying gales and deadly storms he and his crew had been through.

Finally, he concluded his story with the fact that he was part Nanticoke Indian and his great-grandfather had been given the honor of tribal chief for ten years. He explained how the Nanticoke Indians perform an annual powwow in Delaware, and people travel from across the country to see them celebrate. His family learned various native dances and the art of designing costumes. During the festivities he jumped and leaped around the circle of fire, hooting and hollering. In fact, he stated, he still possessed his colorful feathered Nanticoke Indian costume and would gladly share it with them.

Jimmy hunched his shoulders and turned his head towards the truck's window when he heard Captain Jack describe the costume. He snickered. He could only imagine how utterly ridiculous Captain Jack must have looked with so-called 'ferocious' feathers sticking out of his flat head as he frolicked around a campfire.

"Then you know all about Chessie, the Sea Monster," said Claire innocently. Jim jabbed her with his elbow, silencing her.

"I hope you two aren't planning to search for her," he chuckled. "She's an elusive sea monster, that's for sure. And the funny thing is, no living Nanticoke Indian or waterman has ever seen her."

Chapter 5

From the moment Jim and Claire scrambled out the front door of their home to leave for camp, they noticed the junky red van positioned at the end of their walkway. Silver duct tape stretched around the van's doors, handles, and windows fastening it together. Jim gave Claire a confused look, and as they crept closer to the van, he noticed a streak of white paint ending at a bashed-in passenger door.

Placing their kayak and camping gear on the ground near the van, they tried to open the passenger door. The cracked handle snapped and shattered falling to the ground. Glancing around, Jim realized he had to reach inside the open window and use the inside door handle to open it.

"Don't worry about the handle," said Captain Jack as he shuffled towards them. His dark grayish eyes peered at them. With one crooked hand, he pointed to the handle. "You have to jiggle it a little. Then pull and the door will open. The window crank sticks, too. Yank on it a little and it'll work."

Entering the passenger side, Jim wrinkled his nose at the slight smell of fish. Claire sniffed and pinching her nose trying to avoid the fishy smell. Taking short shallow breaths, she climbed inside, but became squeamish when she saw what looked like fish goo splattered throughout the van, decorating the torn crimson seat covers. Pieces of foam thrusting outward made it difficult to sit as she scooted in and sat next to her brother.

"Jimmy, Captain Jack gives me the ..."

"Ssshhh!" Jim nudged her. They sat quietly in the backseat of the creepy, red van while Captain Jack loaded the kayaks on to the roof. Jimmy gazed straight ahead so he wouldn't draw any attention. Then leaning over, he whispered to Claire, "Do you have the book?"

"It's in my bag." She gently touched her faded green duffel bag and feeling its rough texture, she assured herself of its presence.

Captain Jack peeked in the window of the van and grinned at them. "Looks like you two are glad to be leaving." Recently, Captain Jack shaved his gray beard and cut his hair. This new look made his face look sad and droopy like a hound dog, so every time Jimmy looked at him, he wanted to laugh. The captain had even replaced his old tattered captain's hat with a new one.

"Yeah, well, summers are too hot around here and the challenge of kayaking in some unknown waters sounds good," said Jim.

"Let me know when you're ready to paddle some white water. I have just the teacher for you."

"Thanks, I'll let you know." Jim leaned towards Claire and rolled his eyes. He promised his mother he would be more respectful towards Captain Jack. Sometimes he had difficulty keeping his promise. Especially of late, since Captain Jack was now dining with them three times a week. Jimmy cringed at the thought of it becoming a 'permanent' arrangement.

Their mother was beaming as she locked the door to their trailer. She rushed down the path, where her smile quickly turned into a look of concern. Keeping her eyes on the red clunker as she approached Captain Jack, she handed him her bags.

The brother and sister followed their mother's cautious movements as she examined the clunker. She didn't want to disappoint her children by questioning the captain about the dependability of the van. After all, Captain Jack had assured her of the great mechanical condition of the van when he offered it to them. She affectionately smiled at her children.

"Are you ready?" Her voice was strained as she forced the van door open, climbed in, and then slammed it shut.

"Yes," said Jim. Claire agreed and placing the duffel bag under the seat, she nudged it again with her foot, reassuring herself it was in place. Satisfied, she fastened her seat belt. As the van rolled down the road, the wheels seemed to whisper Chessie's name.

Chapter 6

The first day of their trip was uneventful and the children became bored hearing their mother talk on and on of all the positive changes they had made by moving to Florida. Jim slumped down in his seat and played video games to pass the time. Claire gazed out the window, tallying how many cars had Florida license plates. Bored with her activity, she tenderly tapped her mother on the shoulder and asked, "Why is Captain Jack's hand twisted?"

"You mean…why is it gnarly?" piped in Jim.

Their mother ignored his comment. "He had an accident while working on crab boats in the Chesapeake Bay. His hand was crushed when he was repairing his boat in the boatyard. He barely managed to escape from being seriously harmed."

"That's not how I heard it," said Jim. "The guys at the dock said his hand was smashed over an argument about crabbing territory. He was accused of stealing another man's crab pots and his hand was hammered as a warning."

"Jimmy, that's gossip. He told me what happened."

"Like he's going to tell you the truth!" Jim shoved his feet against the seat in front of him, wrinkled his brow into a frown, and resumed playing his video games. His quietness filled the car.

On the second day of their road trip to camp, Jim and Claire secretly scrutinized pictures of Chessie. While they were examining the pictures, their mother stopped at a gas station at **South of the Border** in South Carolina. As she suspected, she had a flat tire.

"What are you two doing?" she asked as she let herself out of the van. Neither Claire nor Jimmy responded. They quietly slipped the secret book back into Claire's green duffel bag. After consulting with the mechanic, she returned to her children.

"We have to leave the van here for repairs," she said. It was obvious their mother was troubled with the condition of the van and now, an expensive repair bill was making her extremely annoyed.

The mechanic directed the family to a restaurant with the shape of a sombrero for a roof. A trio of waiters wearing glistening velvety sombreros and brightly colored, striped serapes were gathered near the restaurant's door, swaying to the lively music. They opened the door and greeted the family as they entered, "Bienvenidos to the Sombrero Restaurant!"

After being seated under a bright orange piñata in the shape of a burro, the family selected their meals. When they finished eating, the trio of waiters began zigzagging through the festive restaurant grinning and singing. "Feliz cumpleaños, feliz cumpleaños!" They rapidly clapped their hands to the rhythm of the song. In the center of the group of waiters, the chef cautiously made her way to their table and presented their mother with a cheery birthday cupcake sporting a lit candle.

June's face flushed bright red and her smiling eyes filled with tears. "Did you tell them it's my birthday?" she asked.

"Well, something had to make you smile today," said Jim. She hugged her children.

Chapter 7

"You two realize we're not dismissing the past or your father. It's just time to move on. We need to have a life and a future. Your dad was a hero...," she said with a tremor in her voice. "He would want us to go on with our lives."

It was quiet in the van. Claire reached over the frayed seat and laid her head on her mother's shoulder. Neither Jim nor Claire felt comfortable talking to their mother about their father's death. It seemed as if the discussions would cause the family to become unsettled. They missed him, but nothing they did or said would change what had happened. Little by little, the silence and sadness passed. Jim focused on his video games. Staring out the window, Claire thought about the kayak camp and what she was hoping to find there.

After crossing the Virginia state line they arrived in Maryland and Claire was the first to spot the Chesapeake Bay Bridge looming in the distance. She strained to look out the window and catch a glimpse of the glistening bay. The anticipation of seeing the Chesapeake Bay added an edge to Claire's voice, as she tugged on Jimmy's sleeve and whispered, "Look!"

Jim tried to hide his curiosity from his sister. Quietly he resumed playing his video games, but Claire was persistent. Turning off the game, he peered out the window after his mother paid the toll. As they approached the bay, he watched the choppy waves churn under the north and south sides of the bridge.

White caps spotted the bay as dark clouds hovered over the water sending an ominous message. The sky was on the verge of turning into a storm. The wind increased and waves pounded the sandbars and vast shoreline. As they scanned the bay, they identified all types of boats. Enormous naval vessels and freighters dwarfed the sailboats, motorboats and workboats. Patiently, the freighters waited to enter Baltimore harbor as barges crawled to the upper bay.

Their mother broke the silence as they continued across the expansive bridge, "We'll stop in Annapolis on the way back," she promised. "There are plenty of museums and monuments to visit. We'll only have a couple of days, but we can pick the museums we're most interested in." The children took no notice to what their mother was saying. Their real interest lay ahead in the Chesapeake Bay.

"The bay isn't always this rough, is it?" Jim asked as he gazed down at the waves. The wind was howling through the swirling waters.

"Doesn't it look exciting?" Claire's eyes were wide open, taking everything in. "I will remember this view forever—won't you? Open the window, Jimmy, and smell the air." The fresh smell of bay water mingled with the smells of sea creatures and bay grasses. She listened to the whistling of the wind as it blew through the bridge.

Jim nodded in agreement with Claire and watched the waves, the white caps, and the small boats that were bobbing like corks in the water. Jim didn't have the heart to tell Claire they might not be able to search for Chessie because of the rough seas and windy conditions. *Everything is connected in nature,* he thought as he watched the turbulent waters. Paddling against the forces of wind and waves would be impossible for them.

Chapter 8

Claire strained to get a view of Love Point as they traveled through Kent Island. Jim questioned if they were ever going to see any wilderness as he watched buildings whiz by.

"This doesn't look like a wilderness to me," he complained. "How many shopping centers and houses can there be?" His anger and disappointed in the landscape was making him grumpy.

All the roads and towns were beginning to look alike to him; it was as if the towns were made from a cookie cutter. He noticed the sameness of the buildings and of the names of stores and restaurants. He began to suspect each store was situated on the same sides of the street in different towns. A drugstore on the left, a fast food restaurant on the right, then a grocery store set back with a huge parking lot in front, and gas stations strategically positioned across from each other. Then the pattern began all over again. Even the colors of the buildings and signs created an annoyance to his eyes. He had to stop looking!

He wanted to get out of the uncomfortable smelly van and into his kayak. Movement, that's what he needed to clear his head. Movement, among calming green trees and grasses, calming blue water and sky, fresh air—that's all he wanted.

"Hang in there, Jimmy. We'll be turning off the highway shortly." June tried to reassure her children. "I know it must be difficult traveling so long. Your camping experience will begin soon, I promise."

Slowly the shopping centers began to fade and eventually, they disappeared. Farms and forest framed the narrow winding country road as they coasted under lush canopies of tall green trees.

They drove through the small fishing town of Rock Hall and turned south, continuing their journey. The winding road led them to a brown and white oval-shaped sign announcing Eastern Neck Island. Once they arrived, they turned off the main road and followed a bumpy gravel road until it ended. Finally, they arrived at the camp and unpacked their equipment.

Feeling the wind blow across the Chesapeake Bay, Jim stood silently by the wetlands and listened to the marsh grasses rustling in the wind. He sensed Claire's energy by his side. She couldn't hold still she was so excited. She kept tugging at his shirt, telling him to look at this and then at that.

He stood gazing at the sunset as vibrant reds, yellows, and oranges wove in and out of the blue sky, changing day into night. Campers singing songs by the campfire caught his attention. A small bat darted across the campfire in the center of the camp, then another. Far above his head, darkness was slowly creeping towards the horizon, exposing billions and billions of stars. The cool night air touched him. He closed his eyes and thought, *This is what I will always remember.*

Chapter 9

Jim and Claire glanced around the camp and noticed a bulletin board with sign-up sheets listing activities the camp was offering. After they were directed to their rustic cabins by a camp counselor, their mother prepared to leave.

"I'll be in the area during the week. I'm visiting Captain Jack's cousin. I won't be far. She's going to teach me how to place crab pots and steer the workboat. Remember to follow the camp rules, you two." She kissed and hugged them. As she strolled thoughtfully down the path, she turned and said, "By the way, Claire and Jimmy, I didn't see any special activities listed. I hope you two aren't planning any mischief." Before they could answer, she walked away.

The campfire's flames leaped into the air in a curling motion, as the camp counselor threw a log on the roaring fire. The campers dispersed after singing the last song. Walking up a footpath to the mess hall, Jim noticed a launching area for the kayaks. He turned on his flashlight and pointed to an opening to the water. Small clumps of bay grass and tall green and brown marsh grass lined the opening, with algae lapping at the water's edge.

Jim asked, "See that little beach off to the side?" Jim and Claire moved carefully down the sandy path to the shallow water. "That's where we'll launch the kayaks on Thursday morning. Early, got that?" prompted Jim. "We'll carry the kayaks to the sandy spot on Wednesday. Make sure you stick your paddle and your life vest in your boat after your last class."

They steered towards the mess hall in search of a bedtime snack. The large wooden building had screened windows situated on three of the sides. Jim and Claire walked in and looked around it, but they felt out of place—no one told them where to sit.

Inside, ceiling fans were whirling over brown picnic tables arranged in rows.

Ice cream machines hummed while counselors made snacks for campers. Campers talked loudly and yelled at each other from across the room, so the mess hall was extremely noisy.

"This reminds me of the cafeteria at school."

"And it's just as loud!" Claire wanted to cover her ears with her hands. "Where do we sit?"

"Claire, Jimmy!" They heard Maggie's voice and stood motionless. She was walking briskly towards them, escorted by two girlfriends.

Chapter 10

"What are you doing here?" asked Jim. His brow wrinkled as he tried not to show he was miserable, completely miserable at seeing Maggie.

"Do you think you're the only one who likes to go to kayak camp?" The two girls standing with Maggie began to giggle. She was disappointed with Jim's unfriendly greeting. They used to be dependable friends—almost inseparable. *Not any more,* thought Maggie.

"We'll see you later, Maggie. Looks like you have some explaining to do." The girls giggled and strolled towards the table, whispering to each other as they glanced back at Jim.

Maggie turned her attention to Claire. "Hey Claire, what cabin are you staying in?" Maggie's black ponytail bobbed from side to side as she spoke. It was obvious she was delighted to see them—especially Jimmy. She stared at him, wishing they could be friends again.

Jim gazed at Maggie. Never before had he met anyone like her. She befriended him when everyone else at school despised him for fighting. When he was suspended from school, she brought him his assignments. It was during one of their many long conversations that she revealed her understanding of what might happen if he continued to be out of control all the time. He never forgave her for what she said.

Claire's eyes darted back and forth from Jim to Maggie. Something made her feel uneasy. "I don't remember, it might be the Eagle Cabin," said Claire. She tugged on Jim's shirt. "Jimmy, are you coming?" They proceeded, walking through the mess hall. "See you later, Maggie," she called.

After picking up their snack, they slid into seats nearest the front door. There they sat watching Maggie and her friends at the far corner, gabbing and laughing loudly.

"Well, this is really great," said Jim. Hunching his shoulders and bending his head down, he avoided looking at Maggie.

"What's wrong? She won't bother you."

"That's what you think. Seeing Maggie is like seeing the Creature of the Dark Lagoon." Jim's mood was gloomy.

They left the mess hall and strolled to their assigned log cabins. Two sets of bunk beds furnished the comfortable looking room. Claire claimed the bottom bunk as her own. Jim told her to grab it right away, because it would be easier to sneak out at night.

After placing her wetsuit in her trunk and preparing for bed, she sat quietly and listened as each girl introduced herself. Then they all began to chatter about the week's scheduled activities. Tired from the long drive to the camp, Claire slipped into her sleeping bag and dreamed of Chessie as she drifted off to sleep.

Jim's cabin was noisy. The boys were tossing a football and tackling one another. Gear cluttered the floor. As his roommates raced in and out of the cabin, he noticed the screen door made a loud creaking noise. He needed to remind Claire they must be quiet on Thursday morning. Putting his clothes away in the storage trunk, he placed his wetsuit on top of his clothes for safekeeping. Catching the football, he joined the other boys.

Chapter 11

On display in the center of the camp courtyard, was a shiny new 17-foot fiberglass yellow kayak with a light-weight paddle. It was the grand prize for the camp's grand finale event, a 10-mile race filled with twists and turns. Different types of obstacles such as floating logs and buoys of various sizes and shapes were going to be strategically placed in the water. Campers were milling around the prize and discussing their possibilities of winning the race. Jim, along with 20 other kayakers, wanted to win in the worst way.

He followed the path to the water and waited for the class to begin. Glancing around, he observed the girls and boys who would be competing against one another. Many of the kayakers were older and bigger than he was. As they introduced themselves, he discovered they were more experienced, too. One kayaker, Jake, was bigger and taller than all the other campers and had won four competitions in the past year. Jim's confidence took a dive when he considered his chances of winning. He felt very discouraged.

"Hey, isn't that guy a show-off?" said Brian nodding towards Jake. Brian shared a cabin with Jim and the two were becoming fast friends.

"He'll probably win the race. Did you see him blast out in front during the tag race this morning? He's hotheaded, too. He was furious when Maggie dropped her paddle after he tagged her."

Jake met up with the two boys. "You're fast," said Jim. "What is your best racing time?"

"It depends, but generally I average fifteen minutes per mile in perfect conditions and no obstacle course. What about you? You look like you're a strong paddler."

"Well, I'm not as good as you. You have a better performing kayak and paddle than I do." Jim glanced at Jake's sleek red kayak and light-weight paddle.

"It helps. See you guys later." Jake left the two boys and joined a group walking to the mess hall.

"We don't stand a chance," said Brian shaking his head. "Let's get something to eat."

The two boys made their way to the mess hall, each lost in his own thoughts about the skills needed to compete in the race. Jim felt awkward about his abilities. He had never competed in an organized race. Most of the time, he was competing against himself, trying to beat his best time.

Jim knew he was the best paddler at the fishing camp, but then again, Maggie had been his only competition. Maggie— what was she doing at the camp and why was she entering the race? As he walked into the mess hall, he was surprised to see her talking to Jake. Her cheeks radiated a glowing red. Smiling, she waved to Jim.

Chapter 12

The campers resumed their kayak lessons in the afternoon. While Jim was learning to improve his paddling technique, Claire attended the intermediate kayak skills class. She was hoping she would learn to roll her kayak. Jim told her he would only take her to search for Chessie if she could survive on the water by herself. Midway through the class, she walked over to her cabin to blow her nose. She couldn't let anybody know the water was hurting her.

"Hey, Claire," Maggie yelled as she raced to catch up with her. "What's up with you two? Why are you avoiding me?"

Claire hesitated. Jimmy gave her strict instructions not to talk to Maggie about anything, especially Chessie. "We aren't ignoring you. We're busy."

"Well, how's the rolling technique coming along? I see your nose is all red. Does it hurt?"

"A little, but please don't tell Jimmy or he won't let me go..." Claire tightened her lips and stepped away. She cast her eyes downward as she pulled on her wet suit and life jacket.

Maggie waited for her to continue. "Won't let you go where, Claire?" she asked patiently.

"Nothing, really, Maggie ... Jimmy will get mad if I even..." Again Claire was talking too much. She tightened her lips, determined not to say another word to Maggie.

"Okay, have it your way. Here's my nose plug. This will help keep the water out of your nose."

"Thanks, Maggie." Claire placed the plug around her neck for safekeeping, and both girls walked in a gloomy silence to their classes.

Later in the day, Jim stopped by Claire's cabin to check on her. "What's that around your neck?" Jim pulled on the nose plug, snapping it against Claire's neck.

"Maggie gave it to me," said Claire as she guarded it. She knew he was going to be furious with her for speaking to Maggie.

"Did you tell her anything? I know she's snooping around."

"Let's go to the mess hall and forget about her," said Claire.

She shuddered at the thought of Maggie interfering with their plans. It would ruin their search for Chessie. Jim was taken by surprise by Maggie's appearance at the camp. It was suspicious, especially since she had never demonstrated an interest in kayak camp. Confused by Maggie's actions, they were determined not to let her get in the way.

Chapter 13

Jim and Claire found a secluded place to examine a map of the Chesapeake Bay. They were finalizing their plans.

"Remember to set your alarm and stuff clothes or towels into your sleeping bag as a decoy. Don't make any noise. Then meet me by the kayaks."

"What if I don't wake up on time?"

"Oh, you'll be able to wake up. The truth is you'll probably never fall asleep," laughed Jim. His mood turned serious. "Don't worry. Just don't let anyone catch you leaving. We'll launch our kayaks approximately three miles from Love Point. So I estimate it will take us about one hour to get there. We'll look around, and then return. We'll be back to the camp by 6:00 am."

"But it doesn't give us enough time to search for Chessie." Claire felt let down.

She was beginning to realize the only reason Jim agreed to the adventure was so he could practice paddling for the race. She began to panic and snapped, "We must have time to look for her!"

"OK." Jim noted the disappointment on Claire's face. "Let's look at the book again and see if we can get a better idea of what we're looking for." He hated to disappoint her, but at the same time he knew they were on a wild goose chase. As they were studying the description of the sea monster, Maggie and Jake appeared. They were becoming inseparable.

"What are you guys reading?" Maggie plopped down next to Claire and glanced at the book in Jimmy's lap. He slowly closed the book as if it were unimportant, so she asked, "How's the nose plug working?"

"OK," said Claire. She was uncomfortable sitting next to Maggie, so she set about untying and retying her shoelaces, hoping to avoid a conversation with her.

Sensing Claire's uneasiness, Jim spoke to Maggie. "Thanks for lending it to her," he said. "I'm meeting some of the guys by the shore. We're going to practice for Friday's race. Do you want to come along, Jake?" Not waiting for a response, he placed the worn book under his arm and strolled towards the shore.

Maggie watched Jim and Jake as they walked away. "Claire, I know you're up to something. Tell me what it is." She waited patiently for her to answer. "Claire, you're about to burst... tell me."

Claire sat quietly. She folded her hands and placed them in her lap. Motionless she looked straight ahead, waiting for the questioning to end.

"I'll find out what it is. Just a warning— you two better not get into any trouble or you'll regret it."

"I have to return to my class now. Thanks for lending me the nose plug." Claire stood up and skipped away from Maggie before she could ask more questions.

Claire liked Maggie most of the time, but now she was beginning to see why she annoyed Jim. *Why does Maggie always look at the worst part of everything?*

Doesn't she realize searching for Chessie is an opportunity of a lifetime? I'll never regret searching for Chessie, thought Claire.

Chapter 14

Wednesday arrived quickly; before Jim and Claire went to bed they reviewed their plans for the next morning. They decided to dress in their wetsuits and slip their pajamas on top. Then they synchronized their watches. They had already packed spray skirts, paddles, a life vest, and dry bags with their headlamps, camera, water bottles, whistle, and binoculars in the bow of their kayaks. Claire was to meet Jim at the launch area where they placed their kayaks. They kept the plan simple.

On Thursday morning, Claire woke and quickly turned her alarm off. Then she stuffed her pillow under her sleeping bag to make it look as if she were still in bed. Finally, she bunched and rolled up her pajamas and shoved them next to the pillow. Glancing around, she turned the knob of the cabin door. It opened easily so tip-toeing, she slipped out of the cabin and closed the door behind her. She paused to make sure the door was secure before she crept away from the cabin. The light from the moon guided her down the footpath where she expected to find Jim waiting.

Jim had a more difficult time leaving his cabin. The boys in his cabin played cards until well after midnight. He thought they would never go to bed. Finally they fell asleep and he put his pajamas on over his wetsuit. Like Claire, he set his alarm. He was afraid he wouldn't wake up on time and he knew he would be lucky to get three hours of sleep. Lying awake in his bed, he thought about his plan to arrive at the kayaks early so he could move them into the water. Eventually sleep took over and when he awoke, he discovered he had overslept. Rushing around his bed, he moved erratically, stuffing his pajamas under his sleeping bag. He knew it looked unnatural, but he didn't care. Quickly and quietly, he slipped out of his cabin.

Meeting by the shoreline was no easy task. It was 4 o'clock in the morning and it took them a while to adjust their eyes to the darkness of the water. The shoreline looked different at night and the details they noted all week seemed to have disappeared into unfamiliar shadows.

The glowing moonlight fell on their faces as they attached the headlamps to their hats, but they didn't turn them on. The stars and moon would be their guide, as they carefully launched their kayaks.

Jim checked with Claire to make sure her whistle was secure in her life vest pocket and her gear was in place.

He looked at the shoreline one last time. With the tide coming in, he knew this was going to cause a problem for her. She would have to paddle with more effort to get through the strong current. For a moment, he had second thoughts. He had to make a decision. "Follow me," he whispered.

Placing his paddle on the back deck for balance, he lowered himself into his boat. First one leg and then the other, and after adjusting his position, he secured his spray skirt. Claire did the same. Using his paddle as leverage, he dug his paddle into the sand and muck and pushed off.

Claire followed, making sure to be quiet. He looked over his shoulder at her and noticed a swift movement on shore. He stopped and listened. Claire was confused and looked at him. "Shhhh..." Not hearing or seeing anything, he proceeded to paddle. Trusting her brother, she followed him out into the Chesapeake Bay.

Chapter 15

The street lights from Kent Island illuminated the sky as they paddled in a westerly direction. Jimmy checked his compass to make sure they were on course. Two more miles to go and they would arrive at Love Point. Claire struggled to keep up with him. She was having difficulty making headway. He slowed down and floated next to her. "You okay?" he asked.

"It's a little harder than I thought."

"Here, come up alongside my kayak and we'll take a breather." He placed his paddle across the deck of her kayak, holding on to her. As Claire rested, Jim noticed the current drifting them backwards toward shore. "Let's go," he whispered. Only the murmur of the wind could be heard.

Then, with less than one mile to go, the wind switched, turning against them and howling wildly as it blew by. The momentum of the sea's swells increased as the wind sped up. Jimmy looked over his shoulder. He started to doubt his decision to chase after a sea monster. What was he thinking? How could he put his sister in danger? She trusted him.

He blinked his eyes, trying to get a better focus on what lay ahead. Suddenly, he saw four-foot waves unleashing on a nearby sandbar. He hadn't thought of investigating the depth of the water they would be kayaking in, and now there was a sandbar in front of them. He knew if they didn't turn around, they would be tossed about in the rough waves.

"Brace yourself, Claire, brace," he screamed out to her.

It was useless. The surf and wind were roaring, so she couldn't hear him. The wind caught his kayak, flipping him in the opposite direction. Leaning to his right and paddling with all his might, he gained control and turned his kayak into the wind. Just as he was about to give Claire directions, her kayak flipped over her head sending her barreling through the crashing waves.

Tossed by the waves, water splashed unyielding on Claire's face, as she leaned from one side to the other, trying to regain her balance. Her paddle was knocked from her hands by the monstrous waves as they continued to break upon the sandbar.

Suddenly, she was upside down in the water. She held her breath and remembering her brother's instructions, she released her spray skirt and pushed her way out of the kayak.

Chapter 16

A wave slammed hard onto Claire's boat, flinging it out of her hands. As it floated away, she bounced to the surface of the water, gasping for air, as her life jacket kept her afloat. Foam was all around her. She could barely hear Jim's muffled voice as the howling storm screamed in her ears.

Claire stretched her legs down, realizing she could stand and was able to balance herself on the sandbar. She looked around. Her paddle was floating far from her, and she couldn't find her kayak. Then a wave pushed her and she lost her balance. Claire nervously called to Jimmy.

Frantically paddling toward his sister, Jim was running the risk of flipping his own kayak. He couldn't find her. The wind blew in a hard, driving rain, so as he searched for Claire, he constantly wiped the water from his eyes and nose. Suddenly, he couldn't believe what he saw.

Before he could warn her, an eerie dark wave, almost ebony in color, came crashing down, kicking her and her kayak into the air. Claire's kayak flew spinning and crashing on top of her head. Jim heard her cry out, and then she disappeared into the waters of the bay. He paddled against the wind with all his might. Again and again, he yelled her name.

Claire held her breath as she felt herself falling listlessly to the bottom of the bay. She squeezed her eyes, shutting them against the saltiness of the water. Raising her hand to her head, she felt the knot where the kayak had landed. Her head was throbbing, but when she checked her nose plug, it was still in place. However, her life jacket wasn't keeping her afloat. A torn strap had loosened her jacket, so she had to struggle to keep it on. Pulling her arms up with all her strength, she tried to swim upwards toward the surface of the water.

The current was stronger than she had realized. It continued to force her further and further into the depths of the bay. Her hair floated around her face covering her eyes, as she could hear the muffling roar of the waves overhead. Again and again she pulled, forcing her arms and legs to move. She couldn't push herself upward any more, so exhausted, she lost the fight. Claire let her limbs go limp and surrendering, she let the current carry her away.

A frightening shadow, jet-black in shape, drifted over her. Bubble … air …breathe, bubble …air …breathe. She let air out of her lungs, hoping to ease the pain. Bubbles flowed from her mouth. What was happening? Why wasn't water rushing into her mouth and nose making her drown? Air bubbles surrounded her. Claire inhaled and exhaled, inhaled ...exhaled... . She glided through the water surrounded by an air bubble. Something grabbed her, dragging her deeper to the bottom of the Chesapeake Bay.

Light radiated from the sandy, muddy bottom and a small bubble appeared around Claire's face, forcing her to take another breath. A powerful whirlpool formed, pulling her past green bay grass and nooks and crannies. Glancing over her shoulder, she shuddered. The glowing eyes of a monstrous beast were staring at her.

"Chessie," whispered Claire. Satisfied she had at last found Chessie of Chesapeake Bay, she closed her eyes and drifted off to sleep.

Chapter 17

Claire opened her eyes and found Chessie's large nostrils positioned in front of her mouth and nose. Chessie began to inhale water into her own nostrils and exhaled air bubbles through her mouth. When Chessie opened her mouth, she displayed two neatly lined rows of little, white dagger-like teeth. Claire cringed as she looked at the scary teeth.

Frightened by the enormous sea monster, Claire thrashed her body about, shoving to free herself, but she didn't have the strength to escape. Hiding her face in the crook of her arm, she avoided looking at the sea monster. She realized that Chessie was her only hope for survival, so she knew she had to be brave. Bracing herself, she opened her eyes. What she saw next surprised her.

Chessie's eyes were fierce-looking, giving

her a cold, eerie look. A pattern of shallow ridges, like the ridges on a seahorse lined her face.

Shiny black scales rippled down Chessie's serpent-like neck. When Claire felt them, they were featherlike, but not soft like a feather in texture. The scales turned from black to shades of dark gray and then returning to a jet-black color to cover her large webbed flippers.

Claire nudged Chessie and tried to speak to her, but her voice was gargled and sounded more like a fearful whimper. She felt powerless and began to tremble. Chessie continued to blow air towards Claire, keeping her alive.

Two small round openings on either side of Chessie's head sounded. It started as a high pitch, almost like a shrill whistle, and then leveled off to a low rumbling hum. Rapid clicking noises followed. Whistle, click, click, whistle. Chessie's sounds echoed throughout the water and then softened to a gentle murmur. Chessie was trying to communicate with Claire.

Claire made another attempt to talk.

"Where are you taking me?" she asked.

Again she whistled and a gentle murmur followed. It was as if Chessie was trying to calm Claire and tell her not to worry.

The sea monster arched her long body. Terrified by what might happen to her, Claire closed her eyes and held on tight. Chessie carried Claire away. Together they traveled into another world.

Chapter 18

Gliding with ease through the bay, she sheared the ropes and buoys holding crab traps. She rocked her tail back and forth, causing a gigantic turbulent force. As the crab traps swayed, they broke into tiny pieces, freeing hundreds of crabs. Each crab scurried away, searching for protection.

Next, Chessie snagged a fishing line, and then another, and then another. Holding the lines in her mouth she snapped them in two with her razor sharp teeth. The fish escaped.

Chessie continued her grip on Claire as if guarding her from the dangers of the bay. Mightily she moved with thunderous speed, plunging deeper into the bay. She was aiming for a dark and mysterious shape.

Below the water, embedded in the sand and mud rested an old shipwreck. As they swam closer, Claire saw a grotto of oyster shells encrusted on the old vessel. Shells were growing upwards and outwards from the large wooden ribs of the partially buried boat.

As Chessie approached the wreck, Claire noticed the ship's cabin was resting in the sand. It was surrounded by a tangle of timber that was rotting away. Broken wooden barrels and crates and remnants of the mast's rigging were scattered in bits and pieces across the splintered deck of the once majestic ship.

Reaching inside the ship's cabin, Chessie gently placed Claire's exhausted and limp body on the floor. Then vanishing into the darkness of the bay, Chessie disappeared.

Claire looked up from the cold wooden plank floor. She gasped for air and found she could breathe in the cabin. It was as if an air pocket had remained in the vessel after it sank over a hundred years ago. The air smelled stale, but she was happy to be breathing. As she looked around, her eyes adjusted slowly to the dimness in the cabin.

Chapter 19

The cozy cabin was built of pine wood and resembled a cheery sitting room found in a small house. Great wooden beams hung overhead and held the cabin together.

Two wooden chairs and a small table were situated in one corner of the room and a small black cast-iron stove was in the opposite corner. On top of the stove sat a black kettle. An oil lantern was positioned in the center of a dusty wooden table, which separated twin light-blue armchairs. Two yellow square pillows embroidered with colorful flowers rested on each chair.

Scattered papers, rolls of charts, and navigation tools were piled high on the large desk. On one of the walls was a golden framed picture of a stately woman, while the other two walls were decorated with paintings of various types of sailing vessels.

Thick heavy red curtains covered the small round portholes located throughout the cabin. The cabin doors were locked tight with a strong rusty metal padlock hanging on the brass handles.

Discouraged at seeing the padlock, Claire pulled her exhausted body up. She carefully climbed on the wooden chair and onto the table, concentrating as she went along. Reaching up, she pulled the heavy curtains away from the porthole. She pounded and pounded the glass until her fist became red and swollen.

"Chessie, please come back," she cried out. Claire squinted, hoping to get a better view out the porthole, but she saw nothing. She pressed her face against the window, straining her eyes to look sideways and then up and down. Her tired eyes could search no more.

A solitary fish passed by the window.

"Chessie, where are you? I need you," Claire whispered as she carefully climbed down from the table. Reaching for the armchair, she curled up on the cushion. She was losing hope. "Jimmy, please find me, I'm underwater...please save me." Hugging the yellow pillow close to her, she began to cry.

"A stowaway on my ship!" a bantering voice called out. The sound echoed throughout the captain's cabin.

Startled by the sound, Claire cautiously raised her head. Rubbing her tired eyes, she couldn't believe what she saw. At the far end of the cabin, near the black cast-iron stove, a ghost flew up into the air and began creeping towards her. Claire cowered in disbelief.

"How did you enter my quarters, you scoundrel? And where did you come from?" The terrifying ghost hovered over Claire, waiting for a response.

Chapter 20

Immediately, Claire noticed the ghost resembled the stately woman in the picture hanging on the wall, except that her face was a ghastly color of gray and very pale white. She was stout and her large round shape made her look very strong. She wore a long flowing dress decorated with colorless flowers. An apron was tied snuggly around her waist. Stringy mangled hair circled her face.

Frightened by what she saw, Claire stood up, her body shaking. She proceeded to walk backwards. Stumbling on the tattered edge of a red carpet, she fell to the plank floor. A feeling of terror rose within her.

In a meek quiet voice, Claire began to explain, "I was kayaking and...."

"No!" boomed the ghost. "Tell me the story from the beginning. What brought

you here?" The ghost pounded her fist
on the table. Only the sound of the table
splintering and cracking into pieces could
be heard.

Claire looked at the ghost with teary
eyes. Taking a deep breath, she thought
of Chessie and her hopes and dreams of
finding her. She thought sadly of her father,

mother, and Jimmy. How could she begin to explain the events that brought her to the Chesapeake Bay? It was complicated, mixed-up, and so unreal. Tired, cold, and hungry, she began her story.

"I'm Claire," she said in a small quivery voice.

"Miss Claire, it's a pleasure to meet you." The pale ghost extended her hand to Claire. "My name is Mrs. Molly Hicks and I'm the wife of Captain Charles L. Hicks, master of the schooner, Molly B."

Claire paused as she wiped the salty trail of tears running down her cheeks. "I don't know where to begin."

"Stories begin at the beginning," explained Mrs. Hicks. She was becoming quite impatient with Claire. She turned, floated to the armchair, and sat down. Picking up her yarn from a bag, she began to knit. "Please begin at the beginning."

With a weary voice, Claire spoke. "My father was a hero. Now he's gone. I miss him. My mother packed a few things and moved us far away from our life, our memories, and our friends. My brother is helping me to search for Chessie. And now I don't know where he is or if he's alive. I just want my brother here... to save me."

Chapter 21

Molly Hicks sat rigidly on the light blue armchair and looked thoughtfully at Claire. "Dear, you're missing the details. Why did you search for Chessie?" By the way Mrs. Hicks said Chessie's name, it was obvious she had a mysterious connection to her.

"I don't know...I don't know. Do you know Chessie? Is she your friend?" Fearful thoughts fumbled through Claire's mind. She feared the trouble she caused with her brother and the trouble she was now causing with Mrs. Hicks. She felt helpless.

"Your heart is shattered, isn't it? You're chasing after a dream. And your dream has disappointed you." Mrs. Hicks peeked at Claire in between knitting and pulling her yarn. "I can see this adventure of yours has not turned out as you planned."

"I'm not disappointed. I found her, I

found Chessie. She's real."

"But now look at you. What good has it done you to find Chessie? Now you're here at the bottom of the bay with me. In a magnificent shipwreck, I might add. Your brother is missing and I suppose your mother is missing, too." Mrs. Hicks sighed as she pulled more yarn from her bag.

"Chessie will take me back home. I know she will."

Mrs. Hicks placed her knitting on her lap and looked directly at Claire. "What were you going to do when you found Chessie? Were you planning to do away with her?"

"What do you mean, Mrs. Hicks? I don't understand." Claire was confused by Mrs. Hicks' disturbing remarks.

"Are you planning to take her life?" demanded Mrs. Hicks as she frowned at Claire.

"Mrs. Hicks, when I think of Chessie, I forget everything else. When I read about her, I have a friend to think about. She's company for me. I spent months dreaming about her and imagining what it would be like to actually see her. My brother, Jimmy, and I made plans together, and now my dream is complete. I know I might never see her again, but knowing she really exists makes me happy." Claire wishfully looked out the porthole, hoping Chessie would return to save her.

"Deep in my heart, Claire, I can tell you everything changes. And with each event or thing that changes, there's an opportunity for something new to begin. Dreaming your life away will not solve your problems, dear. I understand how you feel," said Mrs. Hicks gently. "My husband, Captain Hicks, lost me in a treacherous storm. It was all so frightening when our vessel filled with water and I couldn't escape. Then, in one gentle swoop, Chessie helped settle the vessel."

"But I don't want to stay here. I want my family back. I want to go home." Claire hid her face in her hands.

Mrs. Hicks put her knitting away, and standing up, she reached her hand out to Claire. "Come along. Let me show you something that might change your mind."

Chapter 22

Claire followed Mrs. Hicks to a small door in the cabin. "This door will take us to the hold of the ship. It's the place where we carried our cargo when we sailed," explained Mrs. Hicks as she began to open the door. "Careful, don't bump your head."

"Wait. Can I breathe down there?"

"You'll be able to breathe." The door opened slowly as a bubble of air from the cabin lead the way. Claire walked down the stairs descending into the hull of the boat. Mrs. Hicks lead her to an opening on the first level. Claire was surprised by what she saw.

"Isn't it beautiful?" asked Mrs. Hicks, beaming at the sight. A sense of calm and pleasure radiated from her.

At the very bottom of the hull, Claire gazed at a lovely natural wonder—an underwater oasis. Fish of all sizes, shapes, and colors were swimming in unison to the rhythm of the waves. Eels stretched their heads out from the natural crevices in the bay's thick grassy floor, while clams dug themselves deep into the sand. Jellyfish and rays swarmed the water, as a sandbar shark swaggered in and out of the wreck. Baby oysters huddled together in a nursery of life. Blue crabs scurried along the oyster reef, rushing to hide in the dense, lush bay grass. Each sea creature was living in harmony in this cozy nook of the Chesapeake Bay.

"Chessie has a bigger job to do than worrying about a young girl's dream. Fixing the problems of the bay is a gigantic task."

"What task does Chessie have to do?" Claire's eyes darted back and forth, amazed and pleased at the life on display before her.

"When you traveled with Chessie, did you see all the ugly rubbish floating in the water, with more settled at the bottom of the bay?"

"I was scared, so I didn't notice much." Embarrassed by her own selfishness, she looked away.

"Come with me." She took Claire back up the stairs to the cabin. Closing the door behind her, she motioned to her to stand in front of the porthole. "Look out the porthole and tell me what you see."

Much to Claire's dismay, she saw a tremendous amount of litter. Plastic bags floated freely while rusted cans, broken bottles, old tires, and fishing gear lay scattered on the floor of the bay. But it didn't end there. She peered past the mangled wooden barrels and along the sparse oyster beds to see additional devastation.

A broken lawn chair, discarded shoes and sandals of different sizes and styles, deflated torn beach and water toys, and even an old broken cooking grill could be seen in the grass beds. Claire saw bits and pieces of plastic and metal scattered throughout the bay. Turning her head to the side, she caught a glimpse of rusty metal crab traps and nylon fishing lines with hooks floating aimlessly in the water.

Chapter 23

"I'm not a scientist nor do I have a scientific mind, but I do know that what I see is not healthy for the bay." Mrs. Hicks pale face looked concerned and worried. Then her concern turned to an uncontrollable fury. "Humans are forgetting what's important. Life will be broken without the bay. Birds and bay creatures will disappear. Water will no longer be the giver of life without the bay grass and the oysters to purify it. It's no mystery what's happening here." A tear could be seen in the corner of Mrs. Hicks' eye. Slowly, another one formed, and then another. Placing her apron into her hands, she dabbed the tears away. Slowly her sad, salty tears dissolved her ghost vapor and she disappeared.

"Mrs. Hicks, come back," screamed Claire, horrified to be left alone on the shipwreck.

"Come back, I want to go home. Where's Chessie, Mrs. Hicks? I need Chessie! I need Jimmy…"

The sound of the storm changed to a whimper and the bay's swells lessened. Claire heard the sputter of a motor vibrate over the shipwreck. She looked out the porthole to see if a boat was coming to her rescue.

In the distance, she saw Chessie swimming steadily towards the shipwreck. Her tail formed a huge wave as she swam by. The force of the wave broke on top of the ship's cabin, throwing Claire to the floor. She screamed, reaching with all her might to grab onto something as she was tossed about. The wooden cabin split in two.

A large burst of water crashed into the vessel creating a bubble filled with air. Chessie's webbed flipper broke through the darkness, and grabbing Claire, she swept her up. Together they began their slow ascent to the surface of the Chesapeake Bay. Scared, tired, and shivering from the bone-chilling water, Claire saw rays of light ahead.

Chapter 24

Jim began to dread the worst. Frantically blowing his whistle, he hoped Claire would respond by blowing her whistle in return. He blew the whistle in different directions. He struggled to pull the binoculars out of the dry bag, but the wind was still in control.

"Jimmy!"

Jim glanced over his shoulder and found Maggie and Jake paddling behind him.

Violent thunder threatened, sounding a warning and making it difficult to hear. "Jimmy, where's Claire?"

"I don't know," Jim was visibly shaken and losing hope. Dead tired from fighting the erratic waves and wind gusts, he began to blame himself for putting Claire in harm's way.

"Where did you last see her?" shouted Maggie.

"Over there by the breakers." They paddled closer to the breakers and as they entered, a four-foot wall of water swamped their kayaks, flipping them upside down. Swirling like a whirlpool, the water sent them down into the Chesapeake Bay as a brilliant light marked their path. Jim opened his eyes and thought he saw Claire swimming underwater.

Disoriented, he rolled his kayak and sat upright. Brilliant light from the sunrise over the eastern sky glistened on the white foam left by the waves. The fierce winds finally forced the clouds to advance rapidly towards the west, taking the rain with it. Jim searched for Maggie and discovered the waves had pushed her farther away from him. Jake was to his right, closing in on him. Jim and Jake scrambled to paddle towards Maggie.

"Jimmy, I found Claire's paddle floating in the foam. Have you found her yet?" Maggie was out of breath from paddling against the wind and waves.

"Maggie, what's that blue thing over on the shore?" Jake pointed to an object floating along the shoreline.

"It looks like her kayak blew towards shore. It's blue, right?"

Jim stopped dead. Confused and scared, his eyes scanned the bay. It can't be, he thought to himself. In the distance, a waterman's boat could be heard motoring towards them. On the horizon, he spotted another waterman's boat setting crab traps as it bobbed erratically in the rough wavy water. Suddenly, the motoring workboat came to an abrupt stop. Confused as to what direction to take, he became furious. Swinging his kayak, he paddled towards the shore, deserting Maggie and Jake.

With all his strength, he paddled against

the waves and current. Glancing up, he saw a group of campers and counselors signaling him to paddle in. Meanwhile, Maggie and Jake headed in the opposite direction, moving towards the waterman's crab boat.

What are they doing? Why aren't they following me to the shore? thought Jim. He looked at the shoreline. The buzz of a helicopter whirling overhead broke through the sounds of the storm. Jim looked up and noticed the red strips on the side of the helicopter.

He flipped his kayak around and raced to the waterman's boat. Paddling closer, he watched as a red sling and medic were lowered to the deck of the boat. Once onboard, the medic moved with speed. Then, signaling the helicopter pilot, the sling and the medic were hoisted up to the helicopter. Within seconds, the helicopter banked to the left and headed towards land. Jim approached the boat and saw Maggie and Jake onboard talking to the captain.

"Claire, hang in there," whispered Maggie as she lifted her head to follow the helicopter, tears and rain falling upon her cheeks.

"What were you kids doing out here so early in the morning?" asked the boat captain.

"Searching...for Chessie." Maggie's shoulders quivered as she cried.

Someone onboard threw a braided dockline to Jim when he arrived alongside the crab boat. His face was ghastly white and weary from exhaustion. He brushed his wet tangled hair from his eyes and prepared to tie his kayak to the boat when he heard a familiar voice.

"Jimmy, hand me your paddle." An arm reached out to him. He glanced up. Standing at the stern of the boat was his mother.

Chapter 25

Jim sat down between docklines, ropes, wooden baskets, and marker buoys piled in the waterman's boat. His pale face stared at his mother, searching for an answer. He waited. June had difficulty looking at her son. As the workboat turned toward the docks, Jim hung his head.

Rubbing his head with his hands, he noticed his hands were tired and cramped from gripping the paddle. Blisters had formed and were bleeding. He looked at his mother again. He felt stupid for taking his sister out in the dark without thinking of her safety. His mother didn't say a word to him. He wished she would at least yell at him.

Breaking the silence, he hung his head as he spoke. "She had to search for Chessie. Don't you get it? This is the stuff dreams are made of and dreaming helps you to forget... even if it's for the moment." Looking up at his mother, he continued, "Claire wants to forget her feelings. She wants to forget her heart has been broken. Her pretend world helps her to get through the pain. It numbs her. Don't you get it?" He looked at his mother, his brow furrowed.

His mother's face showed shock as Jim spoke to her.

"You expect me to be her father, her guardian, and her keeper? Well, I'm not. I'm a kid. Claire looks to me as a brother. How was I to know the wind would shift and a storm would kick up?"

Jim needed his father to guide him, but he was gone. He missed his dad. Jim knew his life would be empty if he lost Claire, too. Glancing at the Chesapeake Bay, he avoided looking at his mother. It was too late now. Claire was in the helicopter on her way to the hospital, fighting for her life. He stood before his mother and feeling lost and alone, he covered his face with his tired worn hands, and began to sob.

His mother tenderly placed her hand on his shoulder. She knew there was nothing she could say to console her son. She watched as he struggled with his own anger and guilt. Now it was up them to help each other get through Claire's accident.

"Jimmy, she'll be all right. Don't worry. Maggie found her in time and fortunately, Jake was there to help."

"But I wasn't there," he whispered. His mother covered him with a blanket and sat next to him.

Clear skies and smooth water surrounded them. It looked as if the storm never happened. The crab boat maneuvered through calm waters. Fair weather brought boaters out to the water and they steered with ease in and out of channels marking their way. Flocks of birds skimmed the water searching for food, calling to each other. Jim looked out over the glistening water. He laid his tired head down and fell asleep.

Chapter 26

Eventually, they arrived at the docks and Jim, Maggie, and Jake gathered their gear and loaded the van. No one said a word as they drove through the town of Rock Hall turning towards Eastern Neck Island. Then little by little, the silence passed as they neared the camp. Maggie and Jake spoke of the fierceness of the storm and the excitement when Claire was lifted into the helicopter.

Jim remained silent as he listened to the details of the rescue. Scarcely a word was spoken between him and his mother. The light of the late afternoon lead them down the gravel road to the opening of the camp. Maggie, Jake, and Jim were led into the camp director's office.

The camp director solemnly asked them to leave the camp and to not participate in any more activities. When they went kayaking in the dark without adult supervision, they were violating camp rules. Claire's kayak was found near the camp covered in bay grass. Jim had cleaned her kayak and gathered her gear from her cabin. Then he tied straps around the kayaks and secured them to the clunky red van.

Jim heard the crowd cheering the kayakers as they raced through the final obstacle course of the competition. Frustrated, he pulled hard on the straps making sure the kayaks wouldn't fall off the van as they drove home. Maggie walked towards him. He did not want to talk to her.

"How's Claire?" Maggie asked. Her parents would be arriving soon and she was worried she wouldn't have a chance to say goodbye to Jim. Her mom and dad had explained their disappointment in her decision to go out on the water and yet, at the same time, they were proud she was there to help rescue Claire.

"Mom's with her at the hospital." Jim kept loading the van as he spoke. He couldn't bear to look at Maggie. Too much had happen and he felt awkward talking to her.

"Will she be okay?" Maggie's voice quivered as she spoke. "Aren't you glad your mom showed up in the crab boat? What are the chances of that ever happening again?"

"Claire's unconscious. The doctor is expecting her to wake up at any time. Look, Maggie, I don't want to talk about it."

Chapter 27

Claire opened her eyes and found her mother holding her hand. A warm blanket was wrapped around her, keeping her body warm. The hum of hospital machines surrounded her bed. She shifted her body to make herself more comfortable and found a needle with a tube taped to her arm. She tugged the sticky tape.

"Where's Chessie?" she asked.

"Does your head hurt?" Hearing Claire talk brought tremendous relief to June. Her daughter was going to recover. "You frightened us, Claire. What were you thinking searching for a ...?"

"Where's Chessie?" interrupted Claire. "She saved my life. I need to thank her." Claire began to raise herself out of the hospital bed, but the bump on her head made her feel faint. The doctor arrived at the door.

"Chessie? Claire, do you remember what happened to you?" asked the doctor.

"Yes, I fell in the water and Chessie rescued me. She helped me breathe underwater and protected me by leaving me in the shipwreck with Mrs. Hicks..." Claire placed her hand on her forehead and closed her eyes. Her head ached.

Claire's mother and the doctor exchanged concerned looks with one another.

"Claire, do you remember Maggie finding you in the water? A blanket was wrapped around you to keep you warm. The medic attached a breathing machine and a helicopter took you to the hospital. Do you remember any of that?"

"I remember Chessie guarded me while I was underwater. She blew air bubbles to me so I could breathe." Claire closed her eyes and thought about Chessie. "She made sure I was safe and placed me in the cabin of an old shipwreck where I met Mrs. Hicks. Mom, it's so beautiful in the bay's waters— there is so much life. The sea creatures live together in harmony, where one needs the other to survive. Did you know that? Even the sharks have a purpose. And Chessie helps them all. Did Jimmy see Chessie? Where is he? Is he okay?"

Chapter 28

Maggie, Jim, and Jake cheered Brian on as he crossed the finish line. Jim was pleased Brian won the kayak race. After the race, Jake's parents arrived to take him home. Shortly after that, Maggie's parents drove in. They loaded her kayak in silence and disappointment and left without saying goodbye to Jim.

Standing alone in the center of the camp, Jim watched as the other campers collected their kayaking gear and one by one, they packed their belongings and left with their parents. Finally, Jim received a message from the camp director letting him know that Claire was awake and recovering from her near drowning. Jim had one more night at camp and then his mother would pick him up.

He walked to his cabin and lying down in

his bunk, he thought about his sister and the events on the Chesapeake Bay. What would he would say when he saw her? How would she ever forgive him for what he had done? If she wanted to talk about flipping out of her kayak and the waves taking her away, how could he explain what he saw? His head was spinning with questions he wanted to ask Claire. His mother asked him not to speak about Chessie again. But he had to talk to Claire.

Jim was determined to find out what really happened when she disappeared below the water. He knew, deep down inside, Claire's experience only deepened the mystery of Chessie and the Chesapeake Bay.

Glossary

Kayak – *(n.)* a water vessel resembling a canoe except it sits lower in the water

Paddle – *(n.)* a piece of equipment used to maneuver a boat through the water

Spray skirt – *(n.)* a waterproof skirt used to cover the opening of a kayak.

Wet exit – *(v.)* exiting a boat while upside down in the water

Roll – *(v.)* action of sitting in a kayak and turning it 360 degrees while in the water

Brace – *(v.)* using a paddle to balance a kayak

Turn turtle – *(v.)* when a boat capsizes

9 781936 343942